Written by Sue Graves
Illustrated by Paula Martyr (Linden Artists)
Designed by Blue Sunflower Creative

Language consultant: Betty Root

This is a Parragon book
This edition published in 2004

Parragon
Queen Street House
4 Queen Street
Bath, BA1 1HE, UK

ISBN 1-40542-206-8
Printed in China

Tiger's Spots

A Level 3 Reading Book

p

Notes for Parents

Reading with your child is an enjoyable and rewarding experience. These **Gold Stars** reading books encourage and support children who are learning to read.

There are four different levels of reading book in the series. Within each level, the books can be read in any order. The steps between the levels are deliberately small because it is so important at this early stage for children to succeed. Success creates confidence.

Starting to read

Start by reading the book aloud to your child, taking time to talk about the pictures. This will help your child to see that pictures often give clues about the story.

Over a period of time, try to read the same book several times so that your child becomes familiar with the story and the words and phrases. Then your child will be ready to read the book aloud with you. It helps to run your finger under the words as you say them.

Occasionally, stop and encourage your child to continue reading aloud without you. Join in again when your child needs help. This is the next step towards helping your child become an independent reader.

Finally, your child will be ready to read alone. Listen carefully to your child and give plenty of praise and encouragement.

Using your Gold Stars stickers

You can use the **Gold Stars** stickers at the back of the book as a reward for effort as well as achievement. Learning to read is an exciting challenge for every child.

Remember these four important stages:

- Read the story **to** your child.
- Read the story **with** your child.
- Encourage your child to read **to you**.
- Listen to your child read **alone**.

Tiger had lots of stripes. He had
lots of stripes all over him.

Tiger was very proud of his stripes.
"I'm so stripy," he said.

9

Every day, Tiger went to look
in the pool. He liked to look
in the pool to see his stripes.

He looked this way. He looked
that way. "Wow! I'm so stripy,"
he said.

But one day, Tiger had a big surprise. He looked in the pool, and he looked again. Tiger could see lots and lots of spots!

"Help!" said Tiger. "I'm so spotty!
And I'm so itchy!"

Tiger was sad. He sniffed a loud sniff. His tears fell into the pool. Plop, plop!

"I must get rid of my spots,"
said Tiger. "I'll ask Monkey.
She will help me."

Tiger went to find Monkey. She
was swinging from a branch high
up in the trees.

"Monkey, look at my spots!" said
Tiger. "I'm so spotty and itchy.
Can you help me?"

Monkey looked at Tiger. She laughed and swung to the next branch.

"A spotty tiger! I've never seen a spotty tiger before," said Monkey. "Ask Snake. He will help you."

A spotty tiger!

Tiger went to find Snake. He was
snoozing in the long grass.

"Snake, look at my spots!" said
Tiger. "I'm so spotty and itchy.
Can you help me?"

Snake looked at Tiger. He hissed
and shook his head.

"A spotty tiger! I've never seen a
spotty tiger before," said Snake.
"Ask Elephant. She will help you."

Tiger went to find Elephant. She was busy washing.

"Elephant, look at my spots!" said Tiger. "I'm so spotty and itchy. Can you help me?"

Elephant looked at Tiger. She lifted her trunk and trumpeted loudly.

"A spotty tiger! I've never seen a spotty tiger before," said Elephant. "Ask Orang-utan. She will help you."

Tiger went to find Orang-utan.

"Orang-utan, look at my spots!"
said Tiger. "I'm so spotty and
itchy. Can you help me?"

Orang-utan looked at Tiger's spots.
Then she scratched her head.

"You have chicken pox,"
said Orang-utan.

You have
chicken pox.

"That's why you are so spotty and
itchy. But don't worry, you'll soon
feel better."

Orang-utan made a bed of soft leaves for Tiger. She gave him a long, cool drink. She splashed cool water onto him.

"Try to stop scratching those itchy spots," said Orang-utan.

Tiger lay on the bed of soft leaves.
"I feel a little better," he said.

A few days later, Orang-utan took Tiger to the pool.

"Look in the pool, Tiger," she said. "What do you see?"

Tiger looked in the pool. He looked
this way. He looked that way.

"Wow! I'm so stripy," he said.
"Thank you, Orang-utan!"

Read each sentence. The pictures will help you.

had lots of stripes.

Tiger went to find

looked at Tiger.

lifted her trunk.

looked at Tiger's spots.

Orang-utan made a bed
of soft

Gold Stars

Level 3 reading books are for beginner readers who can read short sentences with help.

- More detailed stories
- Builds essential vocabulary
- Speech bubbles repeat words from the main text
- Lively pictures to support the text
- Sentence review activity

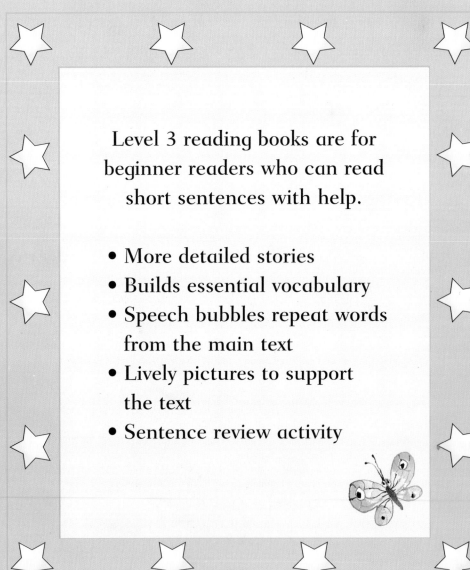